CIRCLE OF WONDER

CIRCLE OF WONDER

A Native American Christmas Story

N. Scott Momaday

University of New Mexico Press

Albuquerque

Originally published by Clear Light Publishers, 1994.
University of New Mexico Press edition published 1999
by arrangement with the author.
3rd UNM Press printing, 2000

Visit the University of New Mexico Press website at:
www.unmpress.com

Library of Congress Cataloging-in-Publication Data

Momaday, N. Scott, 1934–
Circle of wonder : a native American Christmas story /
N. Scott Momaday.
         p.   cm.
Summary: A mute Indian child has an extraordinary experience one
Christmas when, following a figure who seems to be his beloved dead
grandfather, he becomes part of a circle in which he, animals, nature,
and all the world join in a moment of peace and good will.

ISBN 0-8263-2149-6 (cl. : alk. paper)
1. Indians of North America—New Mexico Fiction.
[1. Indians of North America—New Mexico Fiction. 2. Christmas
Fiction. 3. Mutism Fiction. 4. Grandfathers Fiction. 5. New Mexico
Fiction.]
I. Title.
PZ7.M7355Ci   1999
[Fic]—dc21   99-30353
                        CIP

Printed in Canada by Friesens

This book is dedicated to my granddaughter, Skye.

CIRCLE OF WONDER centers upon a world that is so dear to me as to be engraved on my memory forever. I was a boy of twelve when my parents and I moved to Jemez Pueblo, New Mexico in 1946. There was a village of a thousand people, three telephones, two windmills, three or four pickups and no automobiles. But there were horses and wagons. There were cornfields and orchards, there were beehive ovens and brilliant strings of chiles, and there was an ancient architecture that proceeded immediately from the earth. There was an immense and incomparable landscape, full of light and color. And there were people of great dignity and good will and generosity of spirit. It was a place of singular beauty and wonder and delight.

My first Christmas there was beyond my imagining. On Christmas Eve the bonfires were lighted, and sparks rose among the stars. The air was cold and crisp and scented with sweet smoke. The night sky was radiant; the silence was vast and serene. In all the years of my life I have not gone farther into the universe. I have not known better the essence of peace and the sense of eternity. I have come no closer to the understanding of the most holy.

The midnight mass in the pueblo church was a drama of rich and ageless complexity, yet profoundly simple in the story of the birth of the Christchild. The procession to the home of the *patrones* was a quest through time and timelessness, a night journey in the company of ghosts and angels. The stars were close by, all the creatures of the earth were close by, all the living and the dead.
This is the moment of the story of Tolo and the circle of wonder. It was, in the long life of the world, a moment of joy and exhaltation and deep belief. It was the moment of Christmas and of a spirit that transcends time.

N. Scott Momaday

ONCE THERE WAS a poor mute boy whose name was Tolo. In three seasons of the year he lived with his mother and father in the village, but in the summers he went to the house of his grandfather in the great meadow at the foot of the mountains.

Tolo loved above all to be with his grandfather, for the old man was good to him and told him wonderful stories. But when Tolo was still a child his grandfather died, and the boy no longer went to the meadow. Still, he remembered what sort of place it was, and he lived there in his dreams.

He remembered that his grandfather had known the creatures of the mountains. The summer before he died, the old man had taken Tolo to the high rim of the great meadow. They sat at the foot of the mountains, near dark woods of cedar and pine, where they could see out across the long, rolling plain.

As the light darkened in the late afternoon they saw an eagle in the distance. It soared in high, wide arcs above the land, and the setting sun struck a dark fire upon its wings.

At dusk a great bull elk came slowly down from the woods to drink from a spring in the marsh, and it stood like a huge black rock among the reeds in the low mist of the water until the night grew up around it. Then moonlight filled the meadow, and they heard the long wail of a wolf upon the slopes.

Time and again Tolo wanted to tell his parents of what he had seen and heard, but because he had no voice he lived alone with his memories, dreaming. At such times his grandfather came into his thoughts, and then loneliness fell upon him, and he wept.

But now it was Christmas Eve, and there was a great excitement in Tolo's house, for this year his parents were to be the patrons of the Christ child. Even now his mother was preparing a feast for the people of the village, for after the first mass on Christmas morning they would come in procession to pay their respects and to kneel in adoration before the statue of the Holy Infant.

And now, too, his father was building a shrine in a corner of the room where Tolo slept, and Tolo gathered evergreen boughs and made ornaments with which to decorate it.

All day Tolo waited, dreaming of the Christ child. He had worked hard, and he was very tired. At last everything was ready, and it was time to go to the church, for the midnight mass was about to begin.

The church stood at the very center of the village. Its high, thick walls were smooth and earth-colored, and there were three ancient bells above the door.

Inside, the altar shone with the light of many candles. All about there were lovely things to see, paintings and prayer plumes, ribbons and wreaths. At one side of the altar stood a small, perfect tree, its ornaments shimmering in the soft light, and at the other a crêche, in which the statue of the Christ child lay in a bed of straw.

Down the long aisle came
the good people of the village, old
men in beautiful blankets, women
in their fringed shawls, children in
their new Christmas finery.

In one corner, near the door,
a fire roared in an old iron stove.
The metal glowed red, like an
ember, and a cheerful warmth
radiated to all the walls. The
music of bells was everywhere.
How good it was to come into
this holy place from the raw
winter night!

Tolo and his parents sat near the front at a place of honor, where they could see directly into the crêche. The little statue of the Christ child was very beautiful, and for a time Tolo could look at nothing else.

But after a while he began to grow sleepy and to wander in his thoughts. He remembered his grandfather and became very lonely. His loneliness grew so large that he wanted to cry, but at the same time he was glad to dream. It was as if the old man had returned to him. Indeed, his grandfather's presence was there in the church, so real that Tolo wanted to turn around and look for him.

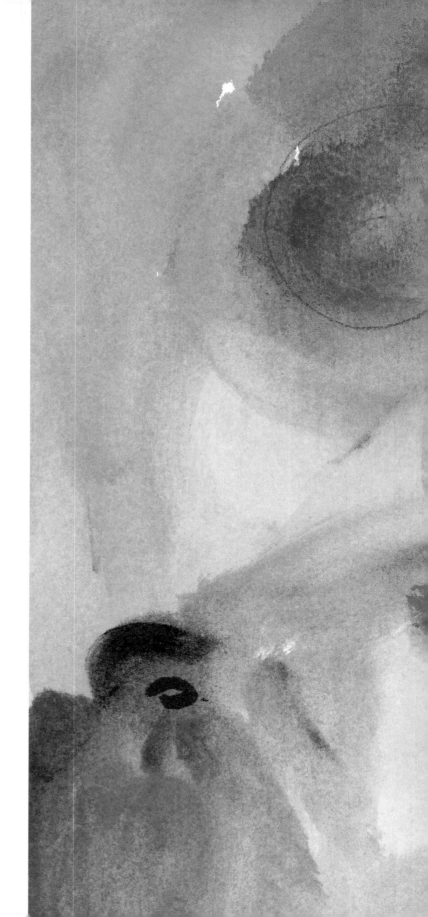

When the mass was ended,
Tolo's mother went to the manger
and took the Christ child in her arms;
she sat with it cradled in her lap, and
Tolo's father sat beside her. Then
the people of the village came
forward to kiss the statue.

Tolo held back for a time, half
asleep, and then he moved to the
aisle. An old man in a blanket was
kneeling before his mother. Tolo's
eyes grew wide, for the old man
appeared to be his grandfather. Yes,
surely it was he! The boy hurried,
trying to call out his grandfather's
name, but he got caught up in the
crowd of people, and then the old
man was gone.

22

Outside, the people were forming the procession. Bonfires had been lighted, and they made a long, bright line through the streets to Tolo's house. The light flickered on the walls of the buildings, and shadows danced about. The night air was clean and cold, and there was a rich fragrance of cedar smoke. Tolo looked everywhere for his grandfather, but he could not find him.

The procession moved away, and Tolo joined at the end. Still he looked all about, running now and then to keep up, for the people were walking very quickly in the cold. Then, far ahead, he caught sight of his grandfather. The old man left the procession and turned into one of the dark streets.

Tolo ran after him, trying again to call out, but when he reached the street, the old man was already at the other end, moving like the shadow of a bird.

He ran, then walked for a long time and became very weary and numb with cold. The lights and sounds of the village were far behind, and the night took hold of him. Still he went on. At last he saw a faint glow in the distance, where the mountains rose up among the stars. As he approached he heard the sharp sound of wood crackling amid flames and smelled a thin, sweet smoke. Lo, there was a fire, like the bonfires of the village, on the rim of the great meadow.

The mountains were covered with snow, and the dark timber seemed to stand upon the slopes like a gathering of old men, huddled and quiet. Tolo knelt down on the bright, warm ground and held his hands open to the flames. "Thank you, grandfather," he said in his heart, but it seemed to him that his voice rang like a bell and made an echo among the trees. The fire filled him with gladness and peace, and he peered into it, dreaming.

After a while he heard something and looked up. The elk entered the circle of light and stood above Tolo, its eyes reflecting the whole of the night. Its antlers shone like shale, and its great body seemed as strong as the wilderness itself.

The sight of the great beast filled his mind with wonder and delight and Tolo dared not move, but he said, "Old Elk, please share with me the real gift of this fire." And again his voice seemed to resound like the wind.

In another moment a shadow moved upon them from the wood. The elk trembled, but only for a moment, and Tolo saw then that there was a long, crooked scar upon its flank, where the teeth of a wolf had long ago cut into the flesh. The wolf drew close and lay down in the light of the fire. The great creature seemed a very motion of the wilderness night, something made of the cold, invisible wind that moves forever among the trees.

Tolo was amazed and said, "Old Wolf, please share with me the real gift of this fire."

There was then a sharp clatter of wings overhead, and only just then, for an instant, did the wolf stiffen and turn, and Tolo saw the ragged edge of the ear, where the talons of a great bird had long ago drawn blood. The eagle dropped down and settled in the firelight. It seemed a spirit of the wilderness sky, holding in its power the very force of the mountain storm.

Tolo felt his heart beating hard within him, and he said, "Old Eagle, please share with me the real gift of this fire."

The hackles of the bird shone like gold in the moving light, and it shifted slightly on its feet, one of which was crooked, having long ago been broken in a trap. Each time he spoke, Tolo's voice rose like a song upon the deep silence of the night.

The boy, the bird, and the beasts made a circle of wonder and good will around the real gift of the fire, and beyond them were other, wider circles, made of the meadow, the mountains, and the starry sky, all the fires and processions, all the voices and silences of all the world.

Tolo knew then that he had been led to the center of the Holy Season. He thought again of his grandfather, who he knew was near among the trees, and of his parents, and of the Christ child, who had come to live the twelve days of Christmas in his home. Never before had Tolo's heart been so full of joy.

The fire burned low, and when again he looked up the wild creatures had gone. He had shared with them the real gift of the fire, and they in turn had given of themselves to him and to each other. Across the great meadow he could see the coming dawn of Christmas Day.

He slept, and when once in the last shadow of the night he awoke, he lay at home in a warm pallet on the earthen floor below the shrine.

The only light in the room was that of a single votive candle; it guttered in the blue glass and cast a soft glow upon the head of the Christ child. Tolo turned and closed his eyes again, and he was no longer poor and mute. His spirit wheeled above the great meadow and the mountains, his loneliness was borne with the wild strength of a great elk, and he sang of his whole being with a voice that carried like the cry of a wolf. *Qtsedaba.*